but it wasn't any use
doodle all the day
a chicken roost
doodle all the day.

For Steven Malk, with affection and gratitude
—D.H.

For Colin and Hank
—C.E.

For information address Disney • Hyperion Books,
114 Fifth Avenue, New York, New York 10011-5690.
First Edition
10 9 8 7 6 5 4 3 2 1
Printed in Singapore
ISBN 978-1-4231-1149-8
Library of Congress Cataloging-in-Publication Data on file.
Reinforced binding
Visit www.hyperionbooksforchildren.com

STAGECOACH SAL
INSPIRED BY A TRUE TALE
By Deborah Hopkinson
Pictures by Carson Ellis
DISNEY · HYPERION BOOKS
New York

I was knee high to a grasshopper when Pa first lifted me up to the shotgun seat.

"Take care, tadpole," called Mama. "Those tiny toes of yours don't even touch the floorboards."

I didn't mind. "Oh, let me hold the ribbons, Pa!

"Giddyap!" I hollered to our four-in-hand.

"Our Sal can sing like a bird," I heard Mama say, "and it sure seems like she wants to fly like one, too."

Mama was **right**. I loved to sit high on the stagecoach seat, the **breeze** in my face and the **thunder** of hooves in my ears.

But the truth is, on this whole wide earth you won’t find anything more dusty and bouncy than a stagecoach journey. That’s one reason Pa liked to have me along.

Of course I helped collect the fares—but I also sang for the passengers. And whenever I belted out “Sweet Betsy from Pike” or “Polly Wolly Doodle,” I kept grown-ups from grumbling and babies from bawling.

Oh, I went to bed
But it wasn't any use
Sing Polly wolly doodle all the day
My feet stuck out a chicken roost
Sing Polly wolly doodle all the day.

Now, I didn't mind helping Pa out, but more than anything I longed to drive myself.

Of course, I didn't mean for Pa to fall into a hornet's nest and get so swelled up he couldn't hold the reins. But as it turned out, that's how I finally got my chance to drive.

Ukiah

"Don't you worry, Pa," I told him.
"I'll get the mail from Ukiah to Willits on time."

"It's a long journey," Pa managed to squeak out.
"No passengers tonight, just the mail."

"No passengers!" Ma flapped her apron in distress.
"You mean she'll be driving alone at night,
with Poetic Pete roaming the countryside?"

Every soul west of the Mississippi knew Poetic Pete. He carried out his holdups by speaking in rhyme. Folks said he was so polite he'd never interrupt a lady, yet he'd managed to rob hundreds of stagecoaches.

"Don't worry, Mama. I'll protect all those letters filled with precious gold nuggets," I declared. "That notorious no-good highwayman will be up against a crack shot. Why, I'm a gal who can plug a nickel from as far as I can see it, and shoot out a rattler's rattles if I care to. Remember, I took first prize in ropin', trick ridin', and shootin'."

"You came in first in singing, too," Mama reminded me.

GIDDYAP!

I hollered.

As I rolled away, Mama waved her apron strings. "Drive, Sally, drive!"

Before you could say "Wells Fargo stagecoach," my team and I were headed over the hills.

To pass the time, I sang my favorite songs.

I could tell from the way my horses' ears pricked up that they liked my singing as much as two-legged critters do. Sometimes I changed the words a bit to fit my four-in-hand and me.

She'll be comin' 'round the mountain
when she comes,
She'll be comin' 'round the mountain
when she comes,
She'll be drivin' four black horses,
She'll be drivin' four black horses,
She'll be comin' 'round the mountain
when she comes.

We went along fine till we came to the loneliest bend in the road. Suddenly a fine gentleman popped out and flagged me down with his handkerchief. The horses started in surprise.

"Whoa!" I cried.

"Please, miss, I'm stranded." He tipped his hat. "Won't you give me a ride to town?"

Now, that fancy suit couldn't fool me. This was Poetic Pete himself, the most polite bandit in all of California.

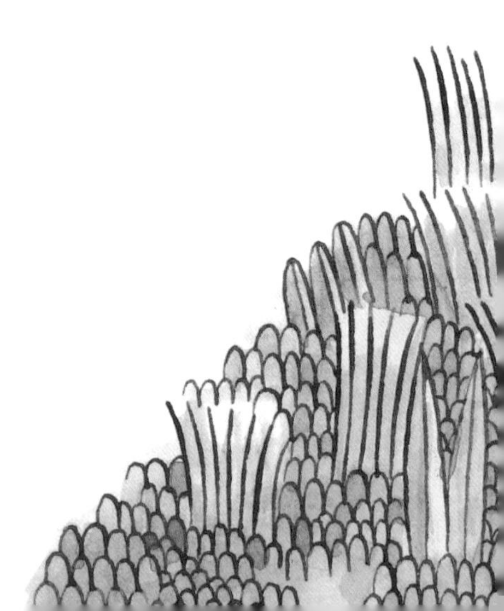

I had to think fast. He was a quick draw with words, I knew. Why, if I let him get the chance, he'd recite a poem like this:

All at once Mama's words about my singing success came back to me.

Thinking fast, I beamed him a big smile. "Sir, I'd be mighty glad to have your company here on the shotgun seat on this fine night. After all, I'm just a merry maid, and these roads are full of bandits."

Poetic Pete climbed up, I cracked my long whip, and off we went.

Well, I knew I couldn't let him say a word or I'd be done for. So I took a good, deep breath and began to sing.

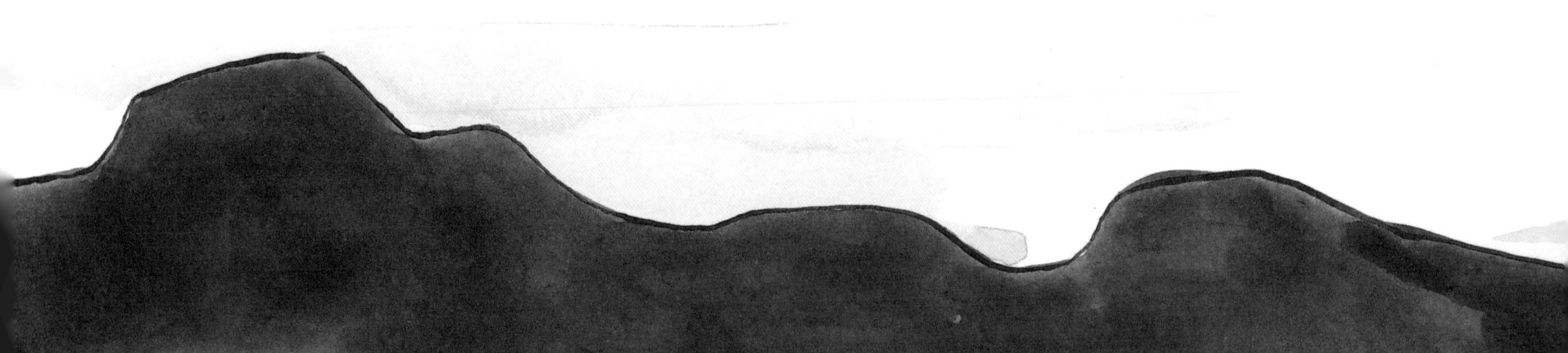

Oh don't you remember sweet Betsy from Pike,
Who crossed the wide prairie with her lover Ike,
With two yoke of oxen, a big yellow dog,
A tall Shanghai rooster, and one spotted hog?

I sang happy songs and sad songs. New songs and old songs. Travelin' tunes and beguiling ballads.

And every time Poetic Pete figured to open his mouth, why, I'd just start right up again:

Oh, I went down South
for to see my Sal
singing Polly wolly doodle all the day
my Sal, she am a spunky gal
sing Polly wolly doodle all the day.

The sun went down, the moon came up, and still I sang. I sang as we bounced around big boulders, down dusty hills, and around teeth-clenching curves.

I was sure anxious to see that morning star myself. When will we get there? I thought in desperation. I was running out of verses—and voice.

Suddenly I felt a heavy weight slump against my shoulder. I'd sung Poetic Pete right off to sleep!

Quick as a cockroach scuttling around a campfire, I whisked out my handcuffs and slipped them over his wrists.

"Wake up, you rhyming robber. The jig is up!" I declared, pulling up to the jailhouse just as the morning sun painted the skies as pink as my Sunday parasol.

And that's the story of how I single-handedly snared the cantoing crook.

As for me, I drove that team many more miles over those mountain roads, singing to my passengers, and delivering the mail safely every time. Folks called me Singing Sal, the Stagecoach Gal, and my exploits were known from here to San Francisco.

I never got robbed, and I never stopped singing:

Delia Haskett Rawson: The Real Stagecoach Sal

When Delia Haskett was so small her feet wouldn't reach the floorboards of the stage, she began riding with her father and begged him for "the ribbons."
—PONY EXPRESS COURIER, *June 1937*

STAGECOACH SAL is a fictional story based on the life of Delia Haskett Rawson. According to records I've been able to find, Delia was the first (and possibly only) woman to carry the U.S. mail by stagecoach in California.

Delia was born in 1861, the daughter of Miranda and Samuel Haskett, pioneers who arrived in California in 1854, settling in what is now Petaluma. Her mother was a teacher. Her father served as sheriff, postmaster, stagecoach driver, coroner, tax collector, and justice of the peace. Delia must have been a lively, high-spirited girl. Known as a local beauty and an accomplished singer, she was also a crack shot, expert rider, and roper.

In a May 16, 1935, article in the *San Dimas Press*, Delia recounted the time she went horseback riding the day after a ball at which she was honored as the most beautiful woman there. Suddenly she caught sight of a salmon trying to swim upstream.

"I dismounted and in my excitement waded right into the stream, clothes and all, on and on, round and round, almost catching it time and time again; finally, after hours, it seemed, I caught the big brute by the tail. What to do with it then? . . . I took a death grip, and cradled the startled salmon in my strong young arms, and succeeded in reaching home unimpaired but very dirty, fishy, and tired."

Delia began driving stagecoaches when she was about fourteen. She became known as "Singing Delia Haskett" because she sang to passengers along the journey.

In this story, Poetic Pete is based on Black Bart, an outlaw known as the "poetic robber" for his polite manners and his habit of leaving a poem behind after each "stickup." Delia recalled that he had ridden in her stagecoach a time or two, although he never robbed her. But she carried a pistol and handcuffs—just in case. Black Bart's real name was Charles E. Boles. Caught after a robbery in 1883, he was sent to San Quentin prison. He was released in 1888 and disappeared soon afterward.

In 1934, when Delia was in her seventies, the Pioneer Stage Drivers of California Association was formed. Delia was elected vice president.

There are many Internet resources for American folk songs. To hear some of Sal's favorite songs, visit the Kids' Pages of the National Institute of Environmental Health Sciences at http://kids.niehs.nih.gov/music.htm

The End

Oh, I went to bed
Sing Polly wolly
My feet stuck out
Sing Polly wolly